B
7-31-05

Level 2.8
Interest (LG K-3)
0.6 pts.

WHAT THE NO-GOOD BABY IS GOOD FOR

BY

Elise Broach

ILLUSTRATED BY

Abby Carter

G . P . PUTNAM'S SONS · NEW YORK

For Harry,

once the no-good baby, now the beleaguered older brother— *E. B.*

For Doug, Samantha and Carter—*A. C.*

Published simultaneously in Canada. Manufactured in China by South China Printing Co. Ltd.
Designed by Cecilia Yung and Marikka Tamura. Text set in OPTI Worcester Round.
The art was done in watercolor.
Library of Congress Cataloging-in-Publication Data
Broach, Elise. What the no-good baby is good for / by Elise Broach; illustrated by Abby Carter.
p. cm. Summary: Tired of all the trouble his no-good baby sister causes, John tells his mother the baby
has to go and she agrees, but as John packs the baby's suitcase,
he realizes there are some things he likes about his sister, too.
[1. Brothers and sisters—Fiction. 2. Babies—Fiction. 3. Sibling rivalry—Fiction.]
I. Carter, Abby, ill. II. Title. PZ7.B78083Wh 2005 [E]—dc21 2003006835

ISBN 0-399-23877-8
1 3 5 7 9 10 8 6 4 2
First Impression

When the no-good baby had been at John's house for
weeks and weeks, and months and months, and more than
half of a year, John decided it was time for her to go.

He was tired of the way
she grabbed his toys and
sucked on them.

He was tired of the way she
cried and cried while he looked
at books or watched a movie.

He was tired of the way she
always fell asleep just when it
was time to play marching band.

He was tired of sharing, and
understanding, and being quiet.

"That no-good baby is good for nothing,"
he told his mother. "It is time for her to go."

"But, John," said his mother, "what would we do without our darling no-good baby?"

"Lots of things," said John. "We could play Go Fish
and nobody would eat the cards."

"That's true," said John's mother.

"And we could bang my drum all afternoon and we
wouldn't wake up anybody."

"I do miss banging your drum," said John's mother.

"See?" said John.
"That no-good baby
is good for nothing.
It is time for her to go."

"I guess you're right," said John's mother.

"I am?" said John.

"Yes," said his mother.

"Really?" said John.

"Really," said his mother. "If that no-good baby is so much trouble, then it is time for her to go."

"Hooray!" yelled John.

"Can you help me pack her things?" asked his mother.

John ran to get a suitcase, but not a very big one, because he didn't want the no-good baby to take too many things with her.

He pulled the no-good baby's clothes from her dresser drawer.

The no-good baby grabbed them and started throwing them around the room.

"See?" said John. "That no-good baby is good for nothing. She is always throwing things and making a big mess."

"I see," said John's mother. "That's not good."

John picked up the clothes and discovered a Cheerio on the floor. "It's only good when she throws Cheerios and makes the floor crunchy to walk on. She is good for making the floor crunchy."

"Well," said John's mother, "I am glad we found one thing the no-good baby is good for."

John's mother took a bag of diapers out of the closet. The no-good baby pulled one out of the bag and squeezed it until it was wrinkly.

"See?" said John. "That no-good baby is good for nothing. She is always squeezing things and wrecking them."

"I see," said John's mother. "That's not good."

John took the diaper away from the no-good baby and put the kitty in her lap. "It's only good when she squeezes the kitty's tail. She is good for squeezing the kitty's tail, because then the kitty likes me best of all."

"Well," said John's mother, "that makes two things the no-good baby is good for."

John found the no-good baby's jingle-bell bear in her crib and put it in the suitcase. The no-good baby grabbed the jingle-bell bear and shook it again and again, squealing loud, loud, LOUD.

"See?" said John. "That no-good baby is good for nothing. She is always making too much noise."

"I see," said John's mother. "That's not good."

"It's only good when she makes too much noise at the library. She is good for making noise at the library, because she's always louder than I am," said John.

"Well," said John's mother, "that makes three things the no-good baby is good for."

John's mother put the no-good baby's blanket next to the suitcase. The no-good baby snatched it and crawled across the room.

"See?" said John. "That no-good baby is good for nothing. She is always taking things and running away with them."

"I see," said John's mother. "That's not good."

John ran after her. "It's only
good when we're having a race.
She is good for having races,
because she always loses."

"Well," said John's mother,
"that makes four things the
no-good baby is good for."

John's mother put the no-good baby's clothes and diapers and jingle-bell bear and blanket in the suitcase and zipped it shut.

"I guess that's everything," she said.

"Yes," said John. "It's time for her to go."

John looked at the no-good baby. She made a wet, bubbly noise and spit dribbled down her chin.

"How far will the no-good baby go?" he asked his mother.

"Maybe to Grandma's house," said his mother.

"That's good," said John. "She'll like that."

"Do you want to give the no-good baby a hug good-bye?" asked John's mother.

"Okay," said John. "Ow! See! That no-good baby is good for nothing. She always pulls hair."

"I see," said John's mother. "That's not good."

"It's only good when Timmy comes over and won't give me back my drum, and then she pulls his hair. She is good for pulling other people's hair," said John.

"See?" said John's mother. "That makes five things the no-good baby is good for. Which is quite a lot. Do you think you will miss her?"

"No," said John.

"Not even a little?" asked John's mother.

"No," said John.

"I think she will miss you," said John's mother. "I think she will miss making the floor crunchy for you, and squeezing Kitty's tail harder than you, and being louder at the library than you, and having races with you, and pulling Timmy's hair for you. She will miss you a lot."

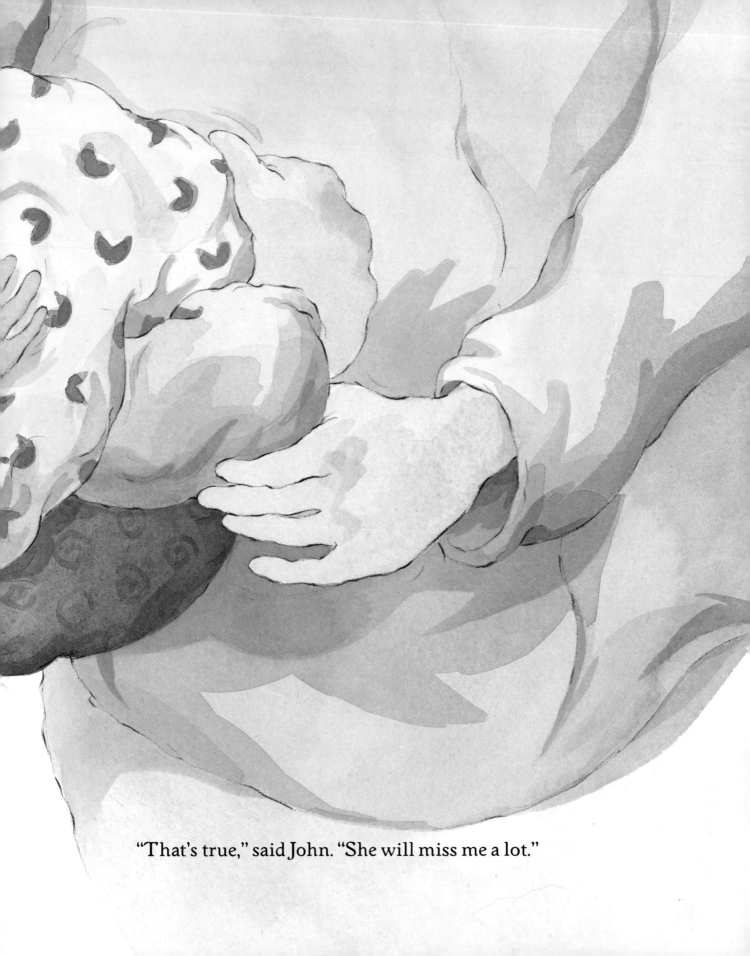

"That's true," said John. "She will miss me a lot."

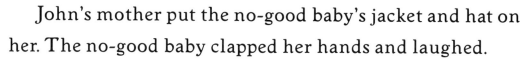

John's mother put the no-good baby's jacket and hat on her. The no-good baby clapped her hands and laughed.

"Is she going to Grandma's forever?" John asked his mother.

"Forever is a long time," said John's mother.

"Maybe she could go to Grandma's just
for today," said John. "For the whole day."

"That's a good idea," said John's mother.
"For the whole day."

"And then will it be just us?" asked John.

"Yes," said John's mother. "Then it will be just us."